TORRID AFFAIRS OF THE HEART ANTHOLOGY

Featuring stories from the following authors:

Ashleigh Cattermole-Crump

Parker Stevens

Raja Savage

S.C. Winters

Scerina Elizabeth

COPYRIGHT PAGE

Copyright © 2022 by Angelic Whispers Publishing
All rights reserved. This book or any portion thereof may not be reproduced or used in any manner whatsoever without the express written permission of the publisher except for the use of brief quotations in a book review.

Printed in the United States of America

First Printing, 2022

ASIN: B09GX8KYPH

Angelic Whispers Romance Anthologies

Table of Contents

TORRID AFFAIRS OF THE HEART ANTHOLOGY 1
COPYRIGHT PAGE 2
THE SEA SWEPT MARQUESS 6
    COPYRIGHT PAGE 7
    ABOUT THE AUTHOR 18
CAPTURING THE VICOUNT 20
    COPYRIGHT PAGE 21
    ABOUT THE AUTHOR 31
    FOLLOW PARKER STEVENS 32
HER LORD'S HIDDEN DESIRES 34
    COPYRIGHT PAGE 35
    PROLOGUE 36
    EUGETE 38
    LORD BAXTER 42
    EUGETE 44
    LORD BAXTER 46
    EUGETE 47
    LORD BAXTER 49
    ABOUT THE AUTHOR 51
    FOLLOW RAJA SAVAGE 52
THE BASTARD DUKE'S MISTRESS 54
    COPYRIGHT PAGE 55
    CHAPTER 1 57
    CHAPTER 2 59
    CHAPTER 3 61
    ABOUT THE AUTHOR 63
    FOLLOW S.C. WINTERS 64
COUNTESS KSENIA'S DARK SECRET 66
    COPYRIGHT PAGE 67
    A MYSTERIOUS STRANGER 68
    SANTUARY IN A STRANGER'S BED 70
    A SPECIAL MESSAGE FROM SCERINA ELIZABETH 73

ABOUT THE AUTHOR 74
FOLLOW SCERINA ELIZABETH 75

ASHLEIGH CATTERMOLE-CRUMP

The Seaswept Marquess

A REGENCY ROMANCE SHORT STORY

THE SEA SWEPT MARQUESS
By Ashleigh Cattermole-Crump

COPYRIGHT PAGE

Copyright © 2022 by Ashleigh Cattermole-Crump
All rights reserved. This book or any portion thereof
may not be reproduced or used in any manner whatsoever
without the express written permission of the publisher
except for the use of brief quotations in a book review.

Printed in the United States of America

First Printing, 2022

ASIN: B09GX8KYPH

Angelic Whispers Romance Anthologies

The darkness outside would soon wane. Even a hint of sunrise meant any one of the thousand roaming eyes could land upon me. I shivered in my cloak, trying to disappear into it. In the distance, where the sun would soon rise, I tried to convince myself that I could hear the trotting of hooves. *This was the right place, wasn't it?* I could barely make out anything in the blackness, but I stood unmoving until the hoof beats caught up to me and I saw a hand reach down from atop the mare. The man's face was covered with a scarf, his eyes the only part of him I fleetingly saw as he hauled me up behind him.

"I was worried you would not come," I whispered to him in the darkness, but he merely grunted and hushed me.

"Not now, there might still be ears upon us."

My father's usually-meek bookkeeper sat stoically ahead of me, and as I held on for dear life my hands found his unassuming robes were hiding thick ropy muscles beneath.

Once we reached the docks, I disentangled myself and fell rather unflatteringly to the ground. As I smoothed the linen and lace of my skirts and cleared my throat to thank him, he galloped away without even a momentary look back. I was on my own.

The ship I was set to board was a small one. Just enough for the merchants returning to the colonies with enough wool and wine to both satisfy the crew and make them a meagre living back in the wild hellhole of their home. All going according to plan, that unknown world would soon also be my backyard. The smell of wet sheep caught in my nose as I covered my face with a cloth to no avail. I bowed my head and stood behind the fishmongers' stall, as instructed in the secret notes that the bookkeeper had smuggled me, and soon a man with a mop of sea-swept black hair and a scowl approached me. He didn't speak a word, instead jerking his head towards the small ship and taking off at a great pace allowed by his thick legs. I only hoped my own sea legs would be as strong.

I hurried along behind his strong shoulders that knocked a path through the crowds.

"Well 'ello love," a voice crackled behind me and I smelt whiskey before I saw a round, mottled face. "Looking for a chaperone, aye?"

"Out of the way!" my black-haired guide gripped him by the collar and tossed him aside as easily as one might discard a bag of sheep droppings. His hand clasped my arm, with surprising care, dark eyes stared deep into my own only for a moment.

"Stay close," he grunted, his voice thick and raspy. He led me through the increasing mass of people, his warm hand remaining on my arm until long after we had boarded the ship.

***

I knew of course that the journey would be long. Under the heaving deck, I was given a small cabin with barely enough room for a bed and a small desk. "Not that a woman needs a desk," the captain had chortled.

As I tried my best to pace my cabin, desperate to calm my racing thoughts, I heard a thump from outside the door. Who was that? Someone trying to enter? Wrenching the handle open with far less caution than I should have had, something heavy fell against me and almost knocked me over. After a startled sound, I saw it was my black-haired friend from the docks.

"What are you doing out here?" I demanded and he looked sheepishly around.

"The men aren't used to having a woman around. They think it's bad luck. I would be remiss if I did not stand guard here, should any of them act on some less than savoury thoughts."

"So, you're just going to sit outside my door for the entire journey?" I didn't know whether to be flattered or annoyed.

The man shrugged and refused to meet my eye.

"At least tell me your name?" was all I could think to say.

"Robert," he answered shortly.

I knew he was right. I had made a hasty and rash decision when I ran from Landsbury Estate. Leaving behind my betrothed, a rotund man in his 60s, I had decided there was nothing left for me there. I had so desperately wanted to avoid marriage to that oaf that I had risked my neck and my virtue by clambering aboard this barely-floating bucket. I slept awkwardly, but I slept, knowing the slumbering mass of dark brooding muscle sat outside my door.

I awoke from a fitful sleep to find Robert had left his post. When I made my way to the kitchen for breakfast I saw him leaning against one of the tables, laughing. Despite the darkness, his eyes sparkled. When they caught mine, I felt a strange rolling in my belly. He wasn't exactly a friendly face, but it was as close as I could find. I walked boldly over to him, noticing several men watching me uncomfortably. As I approached, they averted their eyes, but I wasn't one to care much about their opinions. I had long since felt the only thoughts of oneself that mattered were one's own.

"Good morning, sir," I spoke politely despite the fluttering in my stomach that had little to do with the rolling ocean. The man nodded, turning away towards the kitchen. Not to be dissuaded, I hurried alongside him. "I wanted to thank you for protecting me yesterday."

He grunted again but did not stop.

Before I could say anything further, there was a swirl of waves and we were all knocked from our feet to the slippery wooden floor that stank of oil and rat filth. Robert's strong hands caught me before I hit anything, his body crushed me against him as we struggled against the storm. Around us, the sailors were struggling to stand as the storm that had appeared from nowhere continued to roll the ship from side to side. I could feel hot breath above me and I felt muscles enveloping me as I shuddered and tried to break free. As the two of us stood as one, Robert brushed aside a small patch of dust from the lace of my dress and offered a small smile. Soon the floor was stable enough for the men to return to their flagons. As the men from the deck descended below, rubbing their bruised limbs and muttering in irritation, I was shoved aside and could do nothing but watch as Robert disappeared. Nearby another sailor was lounging on a bench.

"He don't talk much," the man offered helpfully and I smiled. At least someone was speaking to me.

"Why not?"

"Dunno, but he makes good food so we don't complain much."

"He's the cook?" I was surprised. I had always admired the deft hands of our cook back home. I watched him make mama's favourite sago pudding and my brother's bread boats, but my parents always pushed me towards more 'proper' company. I imagined the cook was the only one to notice I was missing, though he was probably glad he would no longer have to cater to my midnight hunger pangs.

"What, that not good enough for you missy?"

"Oh that is not it at all, I myself enjoy reading books of recipes though I was never allowed to do much in a kitchen."

The man stared at me for a second and a cough of laughter emerged. He rolled his round body off the bench with a thump and stood, rather waveringly. He tried to swallow his laughter but succeeded only in hiccoughing himself into a fit.

"Oh that's a good one," he cackled. "A woman reading…" he sauntered off, presumably to find another drink and I was left alone in the dining room, an inch of water threatening to overtake my boots.

I had left the estate with only the clothes on my back and a few personal belongings wrapped in a scarf. I just hadn't been able to bring myself to leave my book collection behind. I had chosen three that fit snugly inside a leather bag and now that the storm had passed, I sat on the deck and flipped one open. It was the first time in many days. I had read no more than a page when I noticed I was catching several strange looks. Several of the sailors were leaning against the railing, their attention attracted either by the sight of a woman reading aboard their ship or the gold and green glint that sparkled on the cover. I tried to ignore them but soon a voice sounded behind me.

"What's in your book miss?" I turned to see a boy who could barely have been older than my brother George who had turned 16 the summer before last. Without an invitation he sat next to me and peered over my shoulder.

"Oh boy, them words are much too big for me," he cackled and I noticed the others were edging closer.

"Would you like me to read it to you?" I asked, finally seeing a crack in the stoic wall of sailors. I cleared my throat and began to read.

Robert had appeared from below, the smell of sweet onions wafting after him and mixing with the deep musky scent I had discovered made my knees a little wobbly. As he walked past me, I felt the brush of his calloused hand against my shoulder, though he gave no indication it had been anything other than an accident. I kept my eyes averted and continued to read from my book to the group who had now assembled around me. I saw him, watching me. I knew the words on the page well by now and I allowed the words to enchant the men at my feet while I snuck several looks at Robert. I knew my voice was stammering but the sailors didn't seem to mind. Robert's eyes flicked over me and I saw a blush of pink spread across his cheeks as he saw me watching. Trying to hide my smile I returned to my book and when I looked up again he was gone. The lurch of disappointment that rolled in my stomach surprised even me.

I thought of the dark-haired cook all night, tossing and turning against nightmares and dreams that ended with me in his arms. He had not arrived outside my door that evening so I rose the next morning with a plan. But as I made my way to the kitchen, my path was blocked by the captain.

"Managing your sea legs are you?" he asked, his tired eyes lingering a little too long on the lace trim of my bodice. Not for the first time I wished I had thought to beg, borrow or steal some men's clothing.

"Yes, thank you."

I made to move past him and his hands reached out and grasped both of my arms. "Where are you going in such a hurry? At least let me escort you to breakfast, it's only polite."

I forced my face into some kind of a smile that apparently appeased him as he let me go and hooked an arm through mine. When we reached the dank, windowless dining area, I craned my neck around the few heads that had beaten us there. The cook was nowhere to be seen, even through the kitchen window, there was no movement. I took a seat at a faraway table, and unfortunately for me the captain took it upon himself to plonk down beside me.

"Oh I'm starving," he hollered, his face dripping with a mixture of sweat and whiskey leaving his body. "Where's that bloody cook?"

No one looked up, apparently used to his outbursts by now, and before I could turn to search for Robert, I felt his clammy, moist hand against my thigh, his sausage-like fingers making their way through the lace. I blustered a little, forcing myself to my feet.

"Apologies, I must return to my cabin. I promised I would bring the book again."

Before the captain could stand, I skittered from the room and out into the hallway. Flustered, I didn't see the figure coming towards me. I felt air beneath me and a familiar set of arms catching me inches from the ground. *Robert*. I could tell who it was by his grunts and the brush of his hair. From somewhere behind us, I heard the captain's drunken voice. "Where's the wretch gone to? Books! What nonsense." Then a crash.

Before I could form any words, Robert had taken me by the hand and was pulling me along the corridor. He shoved me into a small doorway I had not noticed before and I found myself in what must have been Robert's sleeping quarters. The bed in the centre of the room was made neatly, the blankets creased and a table next to it was piled high with books. I was surprised. When I looked at him, he was peeking through the keyhole and I heard the captain's muttering disappearing along the hall.

"He's gone. Probably going to sleep it off somewhere. Bloody drunk."

When he turned to face me, I felt the air leave my lungs. The back of my skirt had backed up against the bed. His shirt was obviously the same one he had slept in and it split open against his chest, revealing lithe muscles and shoulders that threatened to further burst from his clothing. I looked at my feet, unable to control the shiver that ran down my spine as he stepped closer to me. The room was very small, and we were almost touching. Before I could stop myself I reached up and rested my hand against the warmth of his chest. He didn't move, just looked at me, his breathing heavy. Suddenly his body was one with my own and I felt the breath being sucked from my soul, the stiffness of the bed underneath me unnoticeable compared with his warmth. Our mouths hungered for each other until we lay together, tangled and free.

Basking in the flush of my cheeks, a commotion in the kitchens reached our ears. Robert sat up, pulled a shirt on and re-belted his pants.

"I think they're getting impatient." He lowered a gentle kiss onto my head and brushed his hand against my cheek. "Wait here, don't leave."

And he was gone.

I busied myself with the books Robert kept piled high and feeling an odd fluttering in my chest knowing I was in his private space. Where he slept, where he read, where he was only himself. Flicking through the salt-licked pages, I allowed the breeze blowing through the tiny window whisk the hair off my face. When Robert finally returned, he locked the door behind him and produced a large platter of bread, cheese and fruit alongside a large goblet. I gratefully accepted and we sat in silence, nibbling away.

"We're a week out," Robert said suddenly. "From New York, I mean." He was simply stating a fact, we weren't long on this ship before we reached our destination. Well, my destination I realised. His home was here on this ship. Apparently he was reading my mind as before I could open my mouth, his hand slipped into mine.

"I know a man in New York. Every time we dock he begs me to stay, to cook for his guests but I've never had a reason to. Until now…"

I stared at him, crumbs piling up in my lap. "Really? You'd want to leave the ship?"

"Pay's terrible and you've seen the mottled crew. I can see myself living in the city. If you'll be there." His eyes were averted and a blush had spread under the darkness of his hair.

"Of course, I…I…." I felt the heaviness that I had been carrying since leaving home lift from somewhere within my chest. I had been raised knowing my destiny would be marrying for convenience not love. But now, the possibility of love dangled dangerously close. Robert wrapped his arms around me, his breath warm against my neck and we sat for a long time, watching the waves roll outside the window.

"Will you miss it?" I asked. "The ocean."

"Pretty sure this ocean's not the only one," he grinned but I pushed again. I wanted to be sure he wasn't going to regret his choice.

"But are you really sure, truly? You'd want to live in the city…with me?"

He disentangled himself from me and my heart dropped, thinking he had reconsidered. Instead, he collected a small piece of wire that had been wrapped around the base of a candle, holding it upright. He straightened it out and within moments he had twisted it around his finger to form a ring. His hands were shaking as he slipped it onto my finger, and I felt as if I could stay in this room forever and ever with him. But I knew I could not. We had a whole new life to begin.

ABOUT THE AUTHOR

Ashleigh Cattermole-Crump is an author, mother and kitchen witch from New Zealand. She has written stories for adults and children, cookbooks and non fiction but has a particular passion for short stories. She has degrees in history and education, and an interest in feminism, cooking and gardening. Her husband, son and two cats make the writing process slightly more difficult, but also much more fun!

CAPTURING THE VISCOUNT

Parker Stevens

CAPTURING THE VICOUNT
By Parker Stevens

COPYRIGHT PAGE

Copyright © 2022 by Parker Stevens
All rights reserved. This book or any portion thereof
may not be reproduced or used in any manner whatsoever
without the express written permission of the publisher
except for the use of brief quotations in a book review.

Printed in the United States of America

First Printing, 2022

ASIN: B09GX8KYPH

Angelic Whispers Romance Anthologies

Alexandra tapped her foot impatiently as she waited, she hated to be kept waiting. She wondered if anyone would send her to prison for killing him. Her brother's lateness was unforgiveable. She opened the door to the landing a crack and scanned the hallway looking for the familiar bob of her brothers dark head. She slammed the door shut when he failed to appear.

"Alex calm yourself." Her mother said with a patient smile as she smoothed out an imaginary wrinkle in the blue satin of her gown.

"Mother. He is late and he is making me late. This is my engagement party!" Alex said menacingly as she turned on her mother "You can't protect your golden child forever."

"Alex," She laughed sitting up and waiving her hand at her "Quit being so tiresome. Your brother is certainly not perfect, but he is only a few minutes late."

Ales snorted and turned away from her mother's still beautiful face and took a deep breath. Her brother Richard was definitely her mother's favorite, even though Evelyn Reynolds the dowager Duchess of Roth would never lower herself to admit it.

Alex rubbed her forehead and prayed for patience. Her mother had been making excuses for her brother for far too long and now was apparently no different. His string of mistresses and gambling debts were swept under the rug while she was chastised if one stitch was out of place on her needlework. If she didn't love him dearly she might have killed him by now. The truth of the matter was that as flighty and full of vice as he was, she loved her twin brother more than anyone else in the world. She was tired of the whole double standard, but no matter how many times she had this "discussion" with her mother nothing ever seemed to change. Society was as always a gilded cage and she feared that unless she married well she would be stuck in it her whole life. This marriage may not be the one her family liked the idea of but she was running out of time as her third season came to a close. This marriage would at least allow her to keep her status in society.

She stalked to the mirror and ignored the gentle clucking noises her mother was making in the background. She smoothed a plait of her dark brown hair into place. She stared into her own green eyes and tried not to think of her brother's best friend Nathaniel. She had been in love with him since the day he'd rescued her from a mud puddle when she was five. He'd only ever treated her like an annoying younger sister. She always felt a pinch in her chest at the thought of him. The ache was now manageable and she could be in a room with him without flushing or acting stupidly. She wondering if the anxious feeling overwhelming her was really because her brother was late. She always tried to be honest with herself and she hoped she was doing the same now, with such a momentous decision at stake. It wasn't every day one got engaged after all.

The footsteps echoed down the hall and her brother flew into the room out of breath looking quite satisfied with himself. His brown hair, an exact copy of her own was windblown and his green eyes twinkled merrily as if he hadn't a care in the world. He gripped Alex's hands and smiled widely completely ignoring the look of annoyance on his sister's face.

"My darling girl." Richard said with a smile and a kiss on both of her hot cheeks "I'm so sorry I'm late, you look lovely."

"Your flattery will not excuse your tardiness." She said tartly trying not to be drawn in by his exuberant personality. To know him was to love and forgive him anything, something he often used to his advantage.

His eyes began to beg as he hugged her to his chest. The satin of his embroidered waistcoat tickled her face as he squished her to him. "Xandra, don't be cross with me, my horse threw a shoe and I had to walk back to the stable." He smelled like rain and the outdoors and vaguely of horse and Alex already felt her resolve weakening.

"Don't Xandra me," she said pulling back even as a smile spread across her face "you were supposed to be here ten minutes ago, our guests are waiting."

"I am sorry, can you forgive me? Or should I be shipped to the colonies?" His said with a crooked smile as his eyes widened imploringly.

She couldn't help but laugh. "I think the estates rather need you so you may stay, this time." She said with a sigh as her mother tittered happily in the background.

"Brilliant!" he exclaimed as he gripped her hands and kissed them. "But seriously, are you sure this is what you want?" She saw the concern in his eyes and smiled, this was what she had to do.

Of course." She said with as wide a smile as she could manage.

He nodded and led her to the door, even though she didn't miss the tightening of his lips and the look that passed between Richard and their mother. She knew they didn't approve but this was her only choice to get what she wanted.

Alex smiled up at him trying not to acknowledge the dread that crept down her spine. She straightened the skirt of her green gown wondering if she was making the biggest mistake of her life.

****

Nathaniel Rutledge, third viscount of Marlow gulped down the whiskey quickly. The spirit burned it's way down his throat but he barely noticed. He welcomed the fire to push away the feeling of wrongness about this whole night. He nodded at a passing lady but ignored the invitation clear in her eyes. He was off tonight, angry and irritated and he couldn't for the life of him imagine why. He grabbed another whisky from a passing tray and turned his eyes toward the stairs as the music halted. The doors opened at the top of the stairs and he felt his mouth go dry. He went to take a long pull of his drink but stopped as his best friend and his sister slowly descended the stairs. This should have been an everyday occurrence but something in his chest tripped as he watched them descend, well if he was honest watched her descend.

Alexandra nodded her head regally and Nathaniel wondered when she'd grown up. He had seen her of course, nearly every week, but somehow standing under the lights in the ballroom she seemed to shine. Her hair was plaited to one side and lay in long curls over one breast. The soft green of her gown shone in the lights making it seem to glow. The green of her eyes played off the color of the dress seeming to reflect every light in the room.

He took a long glup of his drink and drained it quickly. He wondered how many he would need to dull this feeling inside him. He had a feeling he didn't want to find out. He tried to tell himself that she simply just looked beautiful tonight but he knew that was a lie, he had found himself thinking of her more and more often lately. In fact if he was honest he'd gone to his country estate in hopes of waking himself up from this stupor he found himself in. He'd put it down to his lack of a current mistress or maybe too many late nights at the club, but he knew he had to shake it off. These were not thoughts he should be thinking of his best friends little sister. He found himself wanting things in the dark of night that he had no right wanting.

"Ladies and gentlemen, "Richard said with a wide smile as they came to a stop at the bottom of the stairs "I apologize for my tardiness. My family and I are pleased to welcome you tonight to our annual end of year ball." He didn't move to say more and Alexandra nudged him slightly. Marcus stepped forward form the crowd, looking handsome as ever. Alexandra wished she could find him half as appealing as Nathaniel. Alexandra smiled brightly as the crowd whispered quietly. Richard looked at her quickly and at her nod he smiled at the crowd.

"This evening," Richard said with a slightly forced smile, "I have the pleasure of announcing the engagement of my sister to His grace the Duke of Bennington."

The roar of the crowd was overwhelming but Nathaniel could only hear the rushing in his own ears. Lord Marcus took Alexandra's hand and bowed low over it. His blonde hair fell in his eyes as his lips met her gloved hand and Nathaniel felt his guts turn as she smiled at him with those lovely eyes. The well-wishers rushed forward surrounding the family but Nathaniel stayed rooted to the spot. The world tilted on its access as he saw Marcus Bennington tuck her hand into the crook of his arm. He had been gone three short months and this was not what he'd expected to come back to. The look Marcus sent Alexandra was positively possessive and Nathaniel felt as if his horse had just stepped on his chest.

He turned away looking for any way out, but not fast enough. Richard pushed through the crowd pulling the happy couple with him. "Nate!" Richard asked with a smile that didn't quite reach his eyes. "Did you hear the news?"

"I did," Nathaniel managed to get out softly "I guess congratulations are in order." He said quietly looking at Richard, unable to look directly at the woman who stood beside him. He could feel her green eyes boring into him expectantly but something about the way he was struggling for breath kept him from looking into her eyes.

"They are," Alexandra said stepping forward forcing him to look at her "We are please you could make it tonight, we thought you would continue your sojourn in the country forever."

Nathaniel's brown eyes met her green ones finally and he felt a punch to his gut. Her look challenged him and he realized that this was what he'd been avoiding, the feelings she ripped from him. "I couldn't miss the last ball of the season. I didn't realize there was a surprise announcement today as well."

"We got tired of waiting" Alex said softly, smiling up at him brightly. "So we wanted to surprise everyone."

"It was certainly a surprise to us." Richard said softly meeting Nathaniel's eyes

"A whirlwind romance then?" Nathaniel asked as he raised his dark brow. His eyes searched hers and he felt a connection snap into place. Maybe it had been there all along but he felt its tug from his head to his toe, as if he were finding his true north for the first time.

Marcus's smile didn't reach his blue eyes as he pulled her back and tighter against his side. "Well when I know what I want, I move quickly."

"Maybe too quickly." Nathaniel said tightly as Marcus's arm closed around her waist. He studied the snide expression on Marcus's face and he desperately wanted to punch him. Marcus's family had an estate neighboring their own and he had a reputation in their home county. His rumored involvement with the ruination and death of a lady of good family made him quite dangerous and unsuitable. Nathaniel wondered at Richard for letting such a man near his sister. He was not the kind of man Alexandra should associate with, let alone marry.

"Excuse me sir..." Marcus said quickly as his lips tightened at the accessing look on Nathaniel's face. He stepped forward but Richard stood between the two keeping them apart.

"Come Nate, let's get a drink." Richard said quickly pulling on his arm and leading him away. Nate resisted, meeting Alexandra's eyes for a moment. She raised her chin and dared him to continue, and damned if he didn't want to, if for no other reason than to wipe that smug look off Marchu's face. She lifted one dark brow tauntingly and Nate would have turned back if Richard hadn't' dragged him away.

He heard her sniff across the distance between them as he was hauled off. Something had to be done about this.

The Abduction

Alexandra rubbed her tired eyes and sat down heavily on the bed. She smoothed the white material of her nightdress and pulled her wrap closer. She had a headache that was only getting worse as the minutes ticked by and she was glad that she'd cried off from dinner. All the arrangements being made in the last week were wearing. Most of all the act of keeping a straight, happy face was draining. Alexandra never would have guessed that pretending to be happy would be so hard. Alexandra knew she was doing the right thing, marrying Marcus, but something inside her didn't feel right.

"Perfectly nice night and all I can do is prattle on about "Feeling" odd." She scoffed as she moved to the window seat and sat down rubbing her aching temples. She looked out over the lawn watching the shadows drift across it's perfectly cut green surface. The moon hung over head like a ghostly galleon on a sea of clouds and normally she would have been entranced by its beauty, but tonight she was blind to it's charms. Images of Nathaniel's disapproving face kept swimming before her eyes and she couldn't shake the feeling that there was something she was missing from the whole situation. He normally was a sensible man and for him to dislike Marcus the way he did with no apparent reason was insanity.

"Not that, I've seen him much." She said to herself as she watched a cat meowgi skip across the lawn. The black cat moved like a shadow, it's black fur blending with the night and for the first time she smiled a real smile. Nothing like the fake ones she'd gotten so good at. Nathaniel had been suspiciously absent when she normally would have seen him several times during the week. Alexandra couldn't help but wonder why. He could barely look at her when she did run into him.

A strange noise outside her door had her jerking her head sideways breaking her out of her revelry. Fear slid down her spine as she slid back against the wall. Everyone else was at dinner and save for the servants she was alone. Her heart beat faster as the wood swung in. She wilted back barely managing to keep her scream locked inside but the man who stole into her room was dressed in black and he was huge, his shoulders blotting out most of the low light creeping in from the hallway. He was blocking her only route of escape and she prayed that she could somehow get past him and down the stairs. In that moment she wondered how he got past the footman but she forced herself to focus and pushing down the panic she began to move. She slid along the wall lingering in the deep shadows as the hulking brute spun toward her bed and stalked forward.

Alexandra stayed hidden, becoming one with the shadows that hung on the edges of her room. She almost made it to the door when her foot landed heavily on the loose floorboard by the door. "No," she gasped as the man dropped her bed curtain and spun toward her. She spit out an unlady like curse and took off. Her feet flew as she passed door after door and headed for the stairs down the long hallway. She didn't bother to scream as no one would hear her until she reached the stairs.

Her heart beat loudly as the loud footsteps sounded behind her and time seemed to slow down in those moments as she finally made it to the stairs. She opened her mouth to scream but a large warm hand clapped over her mouth and she was grabbed from behind.

"Let go of me." She screamed from behind the hand he'd clapped over her mouth when he'd hauled her against his chest. "right now!" She flailed and kicked but he wrapped his free arm around her and lifted her off her feet pulling her against the steel of his chest.

The man ignored her and hefted her higher in his arms wrapping his muscled arm tighter around her as he began to stalk down the steps. "you'll be quiet if you know what's good for your." Her captor hissed as he pulled her down the steps. The only sound in the darkness was her muffled screams as she disreguarded him completely and continued to try and scream. She was panicked as she was carried down the hall as if she weighed nothing. He seemed to know just where to go because they barely made a sound. She tried to bite him but he was too quick for her, a wadded up handkerchief ended up being shoved in her mouth as he slid the side door open and carried her out into the night.

Alexandra's mind went mad with fear as the darkness swallowed them. Her captor threw her over his shoulder and her world spun. She saw the wheels of the carriage as they approached and she kicked fiercely as he opened the door and threw her in. She bounced on the seat and tried to make a run for it but again he was too quick and she found herself blindfolded with her hands and feet tied before she could blink. Alexandra landed with a thud on the floor of the carriage and wondered how long it would take anyone to miss her. The man across the carriage sat in silence his arms folded, shrouded in darkness.
The Enlightenment

Alexandra cringed back as the door opened. She raised the vase high above her head and swung the minute the door opened, the vase would have cracked down on the head of the person pushing the door open if not for the hem of her night gown. It's slightly too long length caught on her slipper. Alexandra pitched forward and the vase smashed against the door frame. She gave a small screech as she tumbled forward and hit the floor. She wasn't sure if she was more scared or embarrassed as she was hauled to her feel and planted on a nearby sofa. Alexandra puffed air out and blew the curls out of her eyes as she raised her hands ready to defend herself. She may be a lady but that didn't mean she didn't know how to take a man down. Years of playing with her brother had taught her just where a man was vulnerable, this man would be no different.

Alexandra glared up at the man standing in front of her and stopped. Her mouth popped open as Nate crouched down in front of her. Her shock couldn't have been any greater.

"What is going on?" She asked as her eyes widened at his familiar face. Her hands ran over his features for a moment overcome with worry. "How are you here? We have to get away at once. Have you been kidnapped too?"

Nate smiled at her sheepishly and took both her hands in his. "No I have not been kidnapped too. Rather I'm the one who did the kidnapping."

Alexandra's head spun as a thousand thoughts whirled through her brain. He'd done the kidnaping? What on earth was he talking about? She looked into his eyes as everything started clicking into place. She pulled her hands back and stared at him in shock.

"Have you gone mad? Do you know what Richard and Marcus will do to you? They must think I am dead by now."

"It's what Marcus wanted to do to you, that I'm worried about." Nate said somberly as he stood and sat beside her on the sofa.

Alexandra turned to face him unable to believe what was happening. Never in her wildest dreams would she have believed that Nathaneil was the one who kidnapped her. Nathaniel had always been quiet and reserved and something this atrocious was so out of character for him, so unlike him. It made her question if she knew him at all.

"What are you talking about? Richard and Marcus must be frantic."

"Richard knows." He said in a quiet voice. He was facing her but his eyes kept darting away as if he were ashamed.

"You are mad! My brother would never allow you to kidnap me, I will be ruined!" She hissed as she forced him to face her.

"How do you think I got in so easily? Why no one stopped me? Didn't you wonder why no one came?" He asked softly as he ran his hand over hers.

Alexandra pulled away and paced to the window and back again barely believing what she was hearing. But slowly the pieces fell into place and her heart sank. Richard had done this, had allowed this. How had she been so blind? She felt her blood begin to boil as he came to stand in front of her. She really didn't want to see him now, she really wanted to hurt him, hut them both if she were honest.

Its' for your own good Xandra" Nathaniel said quietly watching her pace.

"You don't get to call me that ever again!" she hissed again as she stopped in front of him. "That is only for people I trust, and what do you mean it's for my own good? Who are you to decide what's good for me."

Nathaniel felt as if he'd been slapped. "I have always wanted your happiness. You can trust me." He said trying to grab her hands "I am as I ever have been, your friend."

"A friend wouldn't go to such measures! One might think you were jealous of my engagement. A friend wouldn't kidnap me, you are surely insane." She growled as she pulled back and stalked to the window turning her back to him. Something about the way he'd called himself her friend rankled inside her. Stabbed some old wound that had finally closed.

"Xandra…" he started as he tried to push down the realization that she was right. Her words rang with truth in his ears and his heart wrenched as he realized that he was jealous. He had always cared about her but now he realized that it was more than he'd ever thought before. The chain that had clicked into place when her engagement was announced tightened and inexorably pulled him closer to her. He reached out for her, reached to put his large hands on her shoulders but she jerked away and held a hand up to warn him off.

Her rejection stung and stilled his tongue. His body burned with electricity and this new knowledge and he wanted to say more but he was suddenly tongue tied. "I came up with the plan and Richard agreed." Nathaniel said finally looking down at his empty hands "It is for your safety."
"My safety?" she said viciously "That's insane! The only thing challenging my safety is you."

Nathaniel went to try again but thought better of it. He strode to the door and opened it with a creak but stopped and stared at her stiff back. "I have only ever done what I thought was best for you. Your brother as well. When this is over you will see that we are trying to protect you."

"Get out." She commanded not looking at him.

Nathaniel sighed and left slamming the door shut. He clicked the lock and heard her screech of anger from inside. He ran his hands down his face and strode off, praying this had been the right thing to do.

***

The runner pounded on the door and Nathaniel opened it. He pulled the missive out of its envelope and handed it to Richard who was slumped on the couch. The last three days of keeping Alexandra hidden had been horrible. She wasn't speaking to either of them and the strain of keeping their whereabouts hidden was getting hard to manage. Marcus was tearing London apart looking for her and Richard had to pretend he was helping. Richard looked like he'd been on a three day drunk whoring binge without the benefits.

"I knew it." Richard said quietly as he studied the note. "The lady is gone but there is nothing but here say to link him to her disappearance. We know the truth but can prove nothing. What are we going to do?"

Nathaniel took a slug of the drink he was holding racking his brain. "Can we ruin him by spreading what we know about?"

"No, we have no proof." Richard grunted wiping his face. "I wish we had another option to this marriage. I cannot let my sister marry this man."

Nathaniel downed the rest of the drink and opened his mouth to answer but stopped short when his footman ran in to the room, hair wild and eye blackening more by the second.

"Sir, she escaped" He said breathlessly "My lady escaped."

Nathaniel and Richard shot to their feet and raced out of the room. Richards horse was gone and Alexandra with it. They shared a look and called the groom. They had to stop her before she did something stupid.

The switch

Alexandra smiled as she guided the horse through the streets. She was heading for her godmother's house, hoping to hide there. She hadn't seen her in months and wasn't really sure if she was at home but this was the safest place. She spurned her horse on and ducked under the gate. The house was silent and Alexandra smiled as she dismounted in the yard. She made her way to the back of the house but halted when she heard the noise behind her. She stopped and turned looking into Nathaniel's eyes.

"How did you find me?" She asked quietly, resigned to being caught.

"I thought of the place you felt most safe and this place came to mind. I remembered that you had always been close to your godmother so I came here."

"Where is Richard?" She asked quietly taking a seat on a bench in the back garden.

"He is currently tearing your home apart looking for you." Alexandra shook her head and met his eyes. She smiled up at him sheepishly. "Well neither of you could really expect me to be kept in that room any longer."

Nathaniel laughed despite his still rapidly beating heart. Alexandra was absolutely right, he didn't know what he was thinking trying to keep her at his house but they both should have known she would escape. There was no way a woman this smart and fiery would stay put anywhere. Her long dark hair was mussed from her flight and though her eyes were downcast they still sparkled in the light. Nathaniel didn't know how he'd missed it all before. He shook his head and stepped closer"You are right. We should have known better."

Alexandra chuckled slightly and noticed that Nathaniel had still put himself between her and the gate leading out to the street. Nathaniel seemed to have given up but he was ever watchful just in case. She liked that about him, his carefulness.

Nathaniel sat beside her and studied her. He breathed out a huge sigh then admitted. "There are a lot of things we should have known."

"Such as?" she prodded quietly as she listened to the birds twitter in the trees. Her heart was beating wildly but she kept her breathing as normal as she could. Something in the air had changed though. Something in the way his eyes traveled over her face left her gasping for breath.

Nathaniel wished he could kick himself for not seeing it, for not seeing her, sooner. He was in love with her. probably had been for years. Now after going through the pain of knowing she belonged to another man he found himself unwilling to play games or wait anymore, he had to tell her how he felt.

"The fact that I should have stopped this engagement instead of letting it happen. "

"Letting it happen? I love that you thought you had a choice."

Nathaniel snorted and pinned her with his eyes "I was so blind to what was in front of me. I took so many chances for granted. I thought that you'd always be here."

Alexandra stood and faced him, her eyes blazing "So you thought I'd always just be here, that no one would want me?"

"NO!" he cried as he stood too "I didn't even know what I wanted until you were almost gone."

Alexandra felt her heart soar as he came closer. His slow movements reminded her of some jungle cat and she felt the flame that was always burning inside her flare to life. Her body was hot and she felt her breath catch as he neared her. The air between then crackled and for the first time in her life, bold Alexandra looked away.

"I...I'm still engaged to Lord Bennington." She gasped as he stepped into her space and trailed his finger under her chin making her look at him.

"Is that what you want?" he asked softly

Alexandra sucked in her breath as his finger ran slowly over her lips. She had wanted him for so long it felt like a part of her now. Her body bent toward his and her clothes felt tight against her straining skin.

"Because it's not what I want." He finished as he tilted her chin up again. His brown eyes blazed as he studied her face. "I want you, I find myself in love with my best friends little sister. He laughed softly at the ridiculousness of it all. "It came upon me like a lightning strike. I can't imagine a life without you in it. I cannot fathom a world in which you belong to someone else. Marry me."

He said the last with a gentle brush of his lips on hers. His lips light but seductive brushed hers tempting her with more. Her eyes slid shut as his mouth took hers, hot and insistent. She lost herself in the feel of his lips and hard body pressed urgently against her own. There was not a force on earth that could have convinced her to break away.

Her eyes fluttered open and she broke the kiss as she met his brown ones. Alexandra was usually not swayed by pretty words but his simple, honest ones moved her more surely than an earthquake would. She smiled up at him and whispered the only word possible. "Yes"

A beautiful smile broke across his face as he cupped her chin and pulled her in. "I love you too." She gasped as she smiled up at him "maybe I shouldn't after you ignored me all these years, but I do." He pulled her in and Alexandra gave in, gave herself over to him as his strong arms wrapped her up in his embrace. She moaned as her hands ran up and down his back pulling him closer.

A throat clearing behind them broke them up and Richard stood leaning against the gate to the back garden. "I take it there is to be a wedding then?"

Alexandra smiled and laughed happier than she had ever been in her life.

The Happy Ending

Alexandra smile out at the lawn wondering at what a difference a month could make. The lights strung up between the trees dance and seemed to her like a dream. She smiled and smoothed her wedding dress down, wondering if she would ever be this happy again.

"There is our beautiful bride. " her brother said as he sat beside her and took a sip of his drink "I would have thought that you would be off with your groom."

"I just needed a minute. It's hard being the center of everyone's attention all day."

"You have never had a problem with that before." Richard snorted as he nudged her shoulder.

Alexandra slapped him lightly and leaned against her as he put his arm around her shoulders. "Don't tell anyone." She whispered quietly "Then everyone will think I have a brain in my head."

"You always were smarter than us all. "He said lightly "I don't know how Nathaniel avoided being caught by you so long. I knew you were in love with him for ages. I'm surprised it took you so long to come up with this idea."

Alexandra smiled up at the older brother she adored and shrugged "I had to do something, or it might have taken him years to realize he loved me." She fluttered her eyelashes at him innocently and he laughed.

"Xandra, you took a big risk using Bennington like that. He really is someone to be careful of. The rumors about the girl are real."

"I know." She sighed, "But I also knew that it had to be someone worth worrying about or he might never have acted. Nice job making him think the abduction was his idea by the way, quite brilliant of you."

Richard laughed softly "it was your idea dear sister, but I do occasionally have my moments. But you are as ever the master of all devious schemes."

"But this time my scheme won me the love of my life."

"Indeed it did," He said with a smile "Life in the ton is sometimes boring and I was tired of watching you moon over him and him being totally oblivious to what was right in front of his eyes."

"I played a dangerous game but it ended up helping me capture happiness."

"It helped you capture a viscount." Richard joked with a smile.

Alexandra slapped his shoulder as Nathaniel walked across the grass toward them. She saw the envious looks from the unmarried women and felt a thrill knowing he belonged to her. He took her hand and helped her to her feet as the fireworks celebrating their marriage burst over the sky. In the brightly colored lights she studied his face and smiled realizing that this was the happiest day of her life.

ABOUT THE AUTHOR

Parker Stevens is an author, mother and preschool teacher who has lived her whole life In Ohio. She has written multiple anthology stories and is the author of Shades of Darkness the first in the Irish vampire trilogy and the solo anthology Spellbound. Parker loves cats, crafts and reading.

FOLLOW PARKER STEVENS

Amazon
https://www.amazon.com/Parker-Stevens/e/B01DRA81B4

Facebook
https://www.facebook.com/parker.stevens.798

Raja Savage

Her Lord's Hidden Desires

HER LORD'S HIDDEN DESIRES
By Raja Savage

COPYRIGHT PAGE

Copyright © 2022 by Raja Savage
All rights reserved. This book or any portion thereof
may not be reproduced or used in any manner whatsoever
without the express written permission of the publisher
except for the use of brief quotations in a book review.

Printed in the United States of America

First Printing, 2022

ASIN: B09GX8KYPH

Angelic Whispers Romance Anthologies

PROLOGUE

All my life, I felt like I had been running. Sold at the age of thirteen to a family that was supposed to take care of me, but abused me beyond belief. Sold time and time again since I turned sixteen because men didn't know how to keep their hands to themselves. My mother taught me that no man should be allowed to touch me without my consent. I never gave them that right.

Now, here I am in another foreign home, to another family that's promised to allow me to live and work there along with other staff members. Miss Adalia was the one that found me and brought me here. Master Carmine and his wife Lady Clarie seem like nice people, that is until Lady Clarie sees her son take an interest in me.

"Miss Eugete, would you fancy coming with me to see my room, and then I can show you yours?" Lord Baxter asks.

"It would be my pleasure, your Lordship." I curtsy, rising and grabbing his outstretched hand.

"Darling, I don't think you should be consorting with the help like that. Miss Adalia will show her to her living quarters, you need to focus on your studies." She commands.

"Now, Clarie, let these children enjoy themselves. Baxter doesn't have any other friends here and I think it would be nice for him." Master Carmine insists.

I can tell Lady Clarie does not like that because she gives a smile that has me stepping back while narrowing her eyes at me.

From that day forward, Lord Baxter and I became the best of friends. He was my first *everything*. He was the only one I decided I would give consent to when the time was right. Only that time never came.

Two years after I moved into the Whitestone manor, Lady Claire had Lord Baxter sent away to complete his studies. I knew that was a lie. She knew we were getting too close to each other and that would not do well. Fancy that, her white son, in love with the little black servant girl.

Who knew five years would pass before I would ever see him again.

EUGETE

Five years later…

"Why does Lady Clarie have us cleaning like this?" I ask Suzette. Over the years, she and I have become close, best friends even.

"Haven't you heard? She is having special guests over for an engagement celebration." She beams.

"I wonder who it could be?" I questioned. Lady Clarie is evil incarnate and I can't grasp the concept that she is having people over for a party.

"I know who it is, but I've been sworn to secrecy." She giggles.

"Oh, you must tell me. Tell me now or else I'll put a hex on you." Dropping my cleaning cloth to the floor to chase her around the table.

"Now, Eugete, you know this will only get us into trouble. You do not have any more room on your back for more whippings." She snorts.

"There is always room for more." I laugh but stop when I see she isn't.
"Don't say that, Eugete. I do not like it when Lady Clarie has you beat just for fun. You need to be on your best behavior, do not do anything that will strike her fancy." She commands.

"Yes, your Ladyship. I shall do my best, but I make no promises." I giggle just as we hear a commotion outside. We share a look between us and take off for the window.

Coming down the driveway is a carriage. That is Lady Claire's guests I am almost certain. We have the house in tiptop shape so I will not fret over that. What I am dying to know is who is in there.

"Let us go outside to have a better look," Suzette suggests. Allowing my feet to carry me outside to the porch, I notice the whole staff, Master Carmine and Lady Claire are all here.

"There must be a King and Queen inside that carriage for the whole house to be out here." Suzette giggles.

"Shh, she will think it is me making such a fuss," I say right as Lady Clarie gives me a pointed look.

"Eugete, my angel, will you come and stand over here by me?" Master Carmine asks.

"Yes, Master Carmine." I let go of Suzette's hand and made my way over to him. I feel daggers piercing my back and look over to see Lady Claire is the one throwing them.

The carriage comes to a stop, the driver steps down from his seat, goes to the side of the carriage, and opens the door. With his hand dangling in the air, I see a petite hair grab ahold of it just before an equally as petite white, blonde-haired woman steps out.

She's beautiful but reminds me of Lady Claire. I hear her snort, which causes me to look over in her direction. She has a sour look on her face which does not help her features.

Hearing more rustling as the next person steps out, I turn my attention back to the carriage and it is like time has stood still. The person stepping out of that carriage is a handsome man and not the young boy I remember.

My word, how he has changed. Gone are the long, flowing curly hairs that would caress the back of his neck, now it is cut short around the edges with a part down the side and one loose curl hanging at the end. I can imagine myself wrapping my finger around that curl as we laugh together under the moonlight.

I continue studying his face until I get to his heart-shaped lips. His eye color and the shape of his lips mirror mine. I remember the first time he kissed me. Lips so soft against mine had me soaring high above the clouds. It was under the old oak tree that is now known as the whipping tree. That tree holds some great memories that I will cherish until the end of time, but it also holds memories that I wish to forget forever.

Those eyes of his were always my favorite. I could look into them and be taken back to the ocean where the green sea glass rocks hide. I look into them now and get lost as if it were just me and him standing here. I watch him watching me and it's searing a hole into my body.

Shaking my head from the daze his eyes always puts me under, I put my head down as I see him taking slow, tentative steps in my direction. Lady Claire's next words stab me right in my heart.

"Darling, we are so glad you are home and you have finally brought your bride-to-be to meet her future family. Are you not going to introduce her to everyone?" She says, with an evil smile gracing her lips.

"Master Carmine, I need to be excused, sir. There is food in the oven that will burn if no one tends to it." Needing to make a swift exit out of there because I can not breathe from what my ears have just heard.

"Yes, my angel, you may be excused." He says kissing my already burning cheek.

"Thank you, master. Suzette, will you help me." My voice is cracking and I know I need to hold it together until I'm alone in my room.

"Of course I will help you, Eugete." She says, coming to my side ushering us away from there.

"Eugete!" I hear Lord Baxter shout, but I can not turn around. Lord help me, if I see his face, those eyes, I will not make it.

"Let her go dear, she has chores to do. Now, do introduce us to your fiance, son." I hear Lady Claire sneer as I take my leave.

LORD BAXTER

My God, she is more beautiful than the first time we met. Her curly long black hair blows in the wind and carries her scent to me filling my nostrils as I inhale. Lavender and chamomile is a scent I have craved since the day I left. Her scent, my sweet Eugete.

Her green eyes shine so brightly as she looks in my direction and takes me in. I've changed over the years and I am no longer the boy that was her first *everything*. I have longed for her for the past five years. There have been other women and I am not happy about that, but they were not my Eugete.

This engagement will not last, because this woman on the side of me is *not* who I will be spending my eternity with. The woman that just fled the room because of my mother is who will and has *always* been mine.

"Mother, why would you do that? I did not want her to find out like that." I spit.

"No sense in prolonging it darling, getting her hopes up. Best to just nip it in the bud, don't you think, Carmine?" She turns, asking my father who is doing his best to ignore her.

"You have just added something else for me to not forgive you about. Daisy, I will show you to your room." I turn to my fiance, taking her hand, leading her inside.

"You will stay there until I send for you," I commanded.

"But why? Your mother was right, you are completely smitten with the help and you are making a fool out of me. I will not stand for this, Baxter." She says stomping her feet.

"You will do well to remember, you do not order *me* around. She was *my* best friend before you came along. I will not throw our friendship away just because we are to be married." I grunt.

"And I will not allow you to make a fool of me either." She says, getting up from where I told her to stay. "I am going to go find your mother and see what she has to say about this." She huffs, walking in the opposite direction.

What the hell have I gotten myself into?

EUGETE

After the fiasco earlier, I am happy to be alone in my room. I do not think I could face the happy couple any longer. Slipping into my white nightgown, I settle into bed hoping sleep takes me. Hearing a soft knock on my door as it slowly opens, has me sitting up to see who dares enter without my permission.

"What are you doing? You can not be in here." I whisper.

"I had to see you Eugete, to tell my side of the story." He pleases.

"It is quite alright. Your mother helped me realize my place in your world a long time ago. Now, if you please, you must leave." I say, giving him my back. When I heard his intake of breath, I knew the mistake I made.

"Eugete, who did this?" He says, rushing over to me, demanding an answer.

"It does not matter. Leave me be Lord Baxter." I beg.

He grabs my shoulder, pulls my nightgown down, and inspects my back.

"I want a name, Eugete." He growls.

"What purpose will that serve for me to tell you?" I ask, shrugging his hand off my shoulder, pulling my nightgown back in place.

He reaches over, grabs my chin, forcing me to look him in the eyes. I must say, I love the feel of his hand on my face.

"Give. Me. A. Name, Eugete." He growls again and it is filling my core with desire.

"Lady Claire gave the orders and either Daniel or Paul would carry it out. Are you satisfied?" I ask not wanting to see his reaction.

"My mother is responsible for this? How long?" He demands again.

"Since the day you left, your Lordship," I informed him.

"Five years? This has been going on for five years?"

"Yes, and you will only make it worse if you do not leave my room unnoticed." My lip begins to quiver.

"There will be no more tears and no more of this treatment. I swear it."

"You do not have a say so here, even Master Carmine does not. Please, you must leave before someone sees you." I beg, letting the tears fall.

"This is not over, Eugete." He promises me as he leans in and places a kiss on my lips.

My sharp intake of breath catches even me off guard.

"I have waited five years to do that." He says, getting up from my bed and walking to the door. "Remember what I said, Eugete." With that, he leaves.

I am in deep cow dung.

LORD BAXTER

Roaming the halls of the house I grew up in, I can not help but think about what Eugete has told me. When I vowed to her that it would not happen again, I meant every word. Making my way back to my room, I decide the only thing to relieve the sexual tension between Eugete and me is to relieve myself.

I will not have sex with anyone other than her any longer. My fiance should get used to the fact that she will become the mistress in this equation, not the other way around. Eugete will and has always been the woman I have loved. Seeing her today sealed that fate for me.

She has me in such a tizzy that it does not take my release long at all. I can not wait until I have her for real. I will ruin her for any other man and make an honest woman out of her in the process. She was *always* going to be mine, no matter what my mother had to say about it.

Speaking of, tomorrow, she and I will have to have a little chat about what has been going on around here for the past five years.

EUGETE

The next morning, Suzette and I set the table for four. As I prepare today's breakfast, I can not help but think about the kiss Lord Baxter placed on my lips last night. If anyone would have caught him in my room, I would get twenty-plus lashes. Not that it matters anymore, I am used to those punishments.

As I began bringing the food out, I found myself smiling from ear to ear when I saw Lord Baxter watching me. My smile falters once I see Lady Claire watching us both, causing me to rush out of the dining room. She does not let me off that easily, because she gets up and follows me.

"Eugete, I can not help but notice how disrespectful you are being in front of my soon-to-be daughter-in-law and *that* will cost you twenty lashes. Suzette will finish here. Daniel, take her outside." She starts barking orders.

Daniel grabs me and takes me outside to a spot I consider my second home. Once there, he binds my hands in rope, throws it around the whipping tree, and secures my hands around the tree as if I am giving it a hug. He then rips open the back of my dress, to expose my already battered back.

"Get on with it." Lady Claire demands, coming around the house to witness my punishment. On cue, Daniel takes the whip from his back pocket and reigns it down across my back. I scream upon contact because this does not feel like the other whips he has used. It feels like there are thorns tearing into my skin.

"Again!" Lady Clarie shouts. "Do not stop until you have given her twenty lashes or you will get forty!"

Not wanting to suffer the same fate, he whips me until he's reached twenty lashes. My back is torn to shreds, blood spills onto the ground and I am crying unwanted tears. She wanted to make sure I screamed for them all to hear.

As Lord Baxter comes running to my aid, I try to stop my tears, but I can not. I am in too much pain.

"Eugete!" He shouts, running up to me. "My sweet sweet girl. What has she done to you?"

"What she always does, my Lord." I manage to whisper as my head hangs low from letting darkness take me.

LORD BAXTER

"Hold on, Eugete," I whisper to her as I untie her from the tree. She falls into my arms, not saying a word. I fear she could be dead if I did not feel her pulse racing as her neck hangs across my wrists.

I try to carefully carry her into the house but it is no use. Either way, I can hurt her while she is unconscious or wide awake. Throwing her over my shoulder, I race inside and make it up to my room. Once there, I send for Suzette to bring me supplies I will need to care for her.

"Hold on my sweet girl. I have failed you so and I swear to you, this will be the end of it." I whisper, brushing her hair off the side of her face. I can see the tears have stained her face, but that does not make her any less beautiful.

Rushing in comes my mother.

"How dare you interfere with her punishment. Do you want to receive the same fate?" She has the gall to ask me as if she has that power over me.

"Mother, you are walking a thin line. No more!" I shout.

"The only way I will stop is if you *marry* Daisy."

Her words cut through me as I looked down at my beautiful girl. I would do anything for her, even if it kills me.

"You win, for now, mother. This is *not* over."

The end to their beginning…

ABOUT THE AUTHOR

Raja has always had a very imaginative mind where she often resides in her free time. That's where all the magic happens.

Writing books from the heart that are developed in a fantasy world where they give you all the feels. What she means when she says fantasy world is that these are just stories intended for you to escape the happenings of real life. Her stories take you on an emotional rollercoaster ride that can go anywhere your hearts desires.

Raja's genre of choice is contemporary romance with a splash of comedy filled with steam and suspense. Her favorite tropes to read and write include enemies to lovers, age gap, bully, paranormal and office romance with a side of domination

FOLLOW RAJA SAVAGE

Amazon Page
https://www.amazon.com/author/authorrajasavage

Facebook
https://m.facebook.com/profile.php?id=106025331833131&ref=content_filter

Goodreads
https://www.goodreads.com/author/show/21422840.Raja_Savage

Instagram
https://www.instagram.com/authorrajasavage/

Tik Tok
https://www.tiktok.com/@authorrajasavage?

THE BASTARD DUKE'S
Mistress

S.C. WINTERS

THE BASTARD DUKE'S MISTRESS
By S.C. Winters

COPYRIGHT PAGE

Copyright © 2022 by S.C. Winters
All rights reserved. This book or any portion thereof
may not be reproduced or used in any manner whatsoever
without the express written permission of the publisher
except for the use of brief quotations in a book review.

Printed in the United States of America

First Printing, 2022

ASIN: B09GX8KYPH

Angelic Whispers Romance Anthologies

Being born into gentry means nothing unless you're male, which as you can guess, I am not. Growing up, there were three rules I had to live by:

1. *Always stay silent*
2. *Be obedient at all costs*
3. *Give heirs*

What a way to live right? That is not what I want for my life. I want to sing and bring joy to the world. That is not the life of a gentry woman though. My name is Vivian DuPree and this is the story of how I went from a gentry wife to a Duke's mistress.

CHAPTER 1

"Vivian, sit up straight, we are not raising you to slouch," the Governess warns.

"Yes, Governess," I meekly reply, straightening my posture as I do.

Governess Mary smiles at me and then goes back to the board teaching us how to complete simple math and writing skills. The education we receive is the bare minimum. If it wasn't for Mama, I don't think we would have gotten one at all. Papa is very "old world", as Mama calls him. Women are meant for three things: silence, obedience, and children.—that's all. So, I try to pay attention in my classes. It helps keep two of Papa's rules easy to follow. I love reading the best because I get to escape into a world full of wonder and mystery.

My sisters and I turn our heads as we hear heavy footfalls. Dread and fear crawl through me as we all turn back to our work, trying to seem busy. The door to the library, where we hold our classes, flies open. Standing there is Papa. He looks frazzled and upset. Oh no, this is not going to be good.

"Vivian Elizabeth, come here please," his bass voice growls as he says my name. Quickly, I stand up and as silently as possible, I walk to him with my head bowed as I get closer.

"Yes, Papa?" I ask with my voice just above a whisper.

"Come with me. You are meeting someone today." He turns his six foot two frame around in the door and marches off leaving me in the doorway with a look of shock on my face. Without even looking back, he yells, "NOW VIVIAN."

I stumble, but quickly catch up and follow. Looking down as I follow Papa, my mind is racing as to whom I could be meeting. I know I am almost eighteen and of marrying age, but Papa said I could wait til I was twenty before he found me a husband.

I wasn't looking at where I was going when I ran into my father as he had stopped outside of his office door. I slowly looked up at him and his eyes were filled with anger and fire. I knew after whatever was about to happen my backside was going to be sore for days.

"Do not speak unless I tell you, and if you even think of not acknowledging the man inside I will make the punishment you are already getting ten times worse," the venom in his voice made it very clear that I was not allowed to make this worse.

"Yes, Papa," I whisper as I straighten myself and my dress. I needed to make a very good impression on the man behind the door. After giving me a once over, Papa nodded, turned and opened the office door.

"Duke Laird, my apologies for the delay," Papa bows and I curtsy for the Duke, "this is my eldest Vivian. She is a very accomplished singer, and piano player. She is currently going through her lessons for painting as well as helping the governess with lessons for her younger sisters."

Duke Laird's soft and gentle footsteps come close enough, I'm afraid to look up. I had no choice in the matter though, as the Duke places two fingers under my chin and brings my eyes up his body and to his face.

As I am forced to look up I see that the Duke is in a gorgeous dark navy blue suit with a maroon red vest underneath. The whiteness of his shirt complements the oliveness of his skin. His hair is a blonde that makes the Sun jealous at how beautiful it is, the only flaws are the light streaks of gray running along his . For a quick second I dare look at his face then just as quickly I drop my eyes back down. His eyes are the bluest I have ever seen, what gives away his age are the wrinkles around them. Even bluer than the ocean paintings I have seen.

"She is gorgeous, Lord DuPree. I can't say I have seen someone with her beauty in the last five counties I have been though. Accomplished in music and is a painter. She seems to have enough girth to bare children to keep the Laird line going. My son will be pleased. I will take her. The wedding will be at the end of the month. Please get her ready and her things. I will take her now," Duke Laird smiles sickly. Grabbing my arm, I suck in a breath to stop me from screaming as he jerks me towards him.

Breathing heavily, his breath smells like onions and horse manure, I try to move my head out of his breath line as he smells my neck deeply, then sighing afterwords. His smile crawls across his face even further, if that is even possible. Trying not to look at him, but it's like a disaster, I just can't look away. His yellowed teeth look brittle and due to fall out, there are a few missing as he opens up to speak to my father.

"She is of breading age is she not?" Duke Laird growls.

"She is Duke Laird. She will bring your son many heirs," my father trembles slightly. There has never been a time in my life that someone, other than my Mama, has made my Papa tremble.

"Good, maybe she will be of good stock after all," Duke Laird jerks me away from him and starts to drag me after him.

I can feel my arm starting to bruise as I try to keep up. It is futile though. He is very long legged and lean so he is quicker than the average man. Yanking one more time as I am falling behind, Duke Laird sneers at me and whisper yells, "Keep up or I will have to carry you. We don't want that do we?" All I can do is shake my head no. He nods in response, letting go of my arm storming towards the front door.

CHAPTER 2

The ride to my *new* home was long and unpleasant. The Duke made sure that I was fully aware that I would be siring heirs for his son. Also that his bastard would also be living with our *family*. The way he talked about this son was full of belittlement and contempt. Which of course gathered my attention.

I stayed silent only nodding to any questions asked and looking out at the countryside as it passes by me. The lull of the road soon soothes me, begging me to sleep. I resist it for a while as the Duke is still awake. I don't know what would happen if I fell asleep. Soon though the lull is to much of a pull. The Duke falls asleep. With feeling just as safe, I let the blackness cover my eyes and fall into a fitful sleep.

****

"Wake up child, we are here," the Duke's deep but nasally voice crosses my ears. A little to close for my comfort. I jerk away, purley by instinct. The look on the Duke's face could kill me where I stood if it was possible for a look to kill.

"I apologize, Duke Laird," my voice is barely above a whisper, and I try to put in as much of a sweetness as I can.

"Better, now make yourself as presentable as possible. You are meeting your betrothed and his *brother*," as the Duke says brother you can see the visible shudder that rocks through his body. That peaks my interest and now I really want to meet this bastard brother.

Straightening myself out, I take a few deep breaths, slowly open my eyes and see Duke Laird already out of the carriage and walking towards the front door. Someone clearing his throat caught my attention as I went to exit the carriage. I looked and the most beautiful man I have ever seen in my life was there waiting with his hand out for me.

His skin was the most delicious chocolate color I have ever seen, it is so smooth and so soft to the touch. He quietly nods and smiles so bright I think I'll faint. I look up at him and sightly curtsy. I smile my sweetest smile, but I am grabbed abruptly by a firm and very strong hand.

"She has come to be my bride, *brother*," a voice almost as sinister as a vipers hiss calls from behind me. I turn to see a man barley as tall as myself. His skin is alabaster white with strawberry blond hair that is pulled back slick. Makes his face look thinned out, like he doesn't have enough skin to cover his face. I try smiling at him, but his brief look at me and I know its going to be as bad here as it is at home. Well, former home, this is my home now.

"I was just being polite to my new sister. As you were late and *father* was not helping, I wanted to give.." he looks at me for help.
"Vivian," I answered meekly.

"I wanted to give Vivian a good impression of our home. Besides, if she is to learn to run the household, someone should show her some kindness before she meets Ms. Sliver," the bastard brother chuckles.

"Ms. Silver may eat her alive, but it looks like she can take it," my betrothed answers snidely.

I walk out his grip and make my way up the grand stairs to the front door. As slyly as possible I sneak a look back to see if the brothers are following. Not surprisingly they are not. They are just staring at me as I walk away from them. I dare a glance and see that the bastard brother is watching me intently like I am something he wants to eat. The other brother is looking at me like he cant wait to slice a knife across my throat then eat my flesh. Little does he know that doesn't scare me.

I walk up to the giant doors, as they slowly open up for me. On the other side is an older gentleman who has more hair on his face than the top of his head. His smile was small but sweet, bowing as I entered he then guestered to my right and I slowly walked that way and waited as I heard the brothers coming in behind me talking very loudly.

They walk on by like none of us are here. I sighed lightly so neither of them could hear me. The bastard brother looked back and smiled at me over his shoulder. I looked away as quickly as possible. I am here to marry the other brother.

"This way ma'am," the butler from before lightly touches my arm and points me to the stairs that are on the left side of the grand entryway. I nod and follow slowly.

CHAPTER 3

The walk to my new room was silent and yet refreshing. I was able to look at the beautiful paintings and nicknacks that cover the walls, floors and tables. I keep the butler in sight as I slow so I don't get lost, but taking my time to try and memorize the way we are going as well as what rooms are what as we pass quite a few.

We stop in front of a door that is a dark oak with the most beautiful design engraved on it. The engraving is soft and pretty but still shows a lot of power and wealth. I slowly reach out to open the door, The shock I receive when a slap hits my wrist startles me. Looking down I see a small ruler is still there. Following the line of the ruler is a woman who looks to be in her late thirties to early forties. Her raven black hair, is slicked back into a tight bun that the skin on her face is so taught it looks like she used glue on her face.

"You never open your own door. As you will be becoming the next duchess you will need to gt used to having others do things for you. I am Ms. Silver. I am the housekeeper and your lady-in-waiting. Anything you need will be gotten and ran through and by me," her voice grated on my nerves. I should be able to open my own door. Instead of arguing I just nod and wait for someone else to open my door. The butler slowly reached for the door, opening it up for me.

"Thank you," I pause waiting for a name from the butler.

"Morton ma'am," he answers shortly. His eyes slide over to Ms. Silver then back to the ground. He bows to us both and then quietly exits.

Calling after him, "Thank you Morton." I see Ms. Silver shake her head at me. Wether she likes it or not, I am going to at least be polite to the poor man.

"You have a few hours til dinner where your presence is required. I will come back and help you and get ready. You have free reign of this wing of the house, I must escort the rest you through. Now rest, your journey must have been tiring," Ms. Silver nods but quickly leaves before I could ask any questions.

****

As promised Ms. Silver showed up and woke me from my sleep. I was washed, patted down, and dressed in what seemed like minutes. Ms. Silver is very effective but abrupt. The walk down the hallways to the dining room we were silent.

I tried to remember which hallways we went down, but Ms. Silver is to quick. I swear she was a ninja in another life. I giggle silently to myself at my thought. Ms. Silver abruptly stops, spins and looks at me. I look back at her without blinking. She may have intimidated her way into this position, but as the lady of the house, I will not be intimated.

She gestures towards a door and I stood there waiting. Ms. Silver nodded to me in approval, going to open the door. I wait for the door to fully open before I enter. The room looks like a ballroom mixed with a throne room. To the left is a dias' with four stairs and four chairs sitting on top of it. One big one in the middle, one on the left and two on the right. The wall in front of me is floor to ceiling window with a view of a garden. The other walls are gold filigree on top of an off white base, bordered with a massive gold frame. In the middle of the floor is a table that could fit forty, but now it only sits four.

Sitting at the head of the table is Duke Laird, to his right is my betrothed, and to his left is the bastard son. I silently walk to the table trying hard as I might to not make any sound. Alas the small clicks and clacks of my shoes hitting the granite floor warns them of my arrival. I will need to get with Ms. Silver to get me softer footed shoes.

Duke Laird rises when I get close enough to the table and walks to the chair beside my future husband. I curtsy to him and graciously thank him for helping me with my seat. I look down at the table as I was for instructions to be given, but none do. Daring to look up I see that Duke Laird has one of his sly smiles and is looking at me.

"My dear, you do not need to look at the table. We would like to see your beautiful face," he pauses to get a look that lingers a little to long before he clears his throat and continues speaking, "My son, Preston, is your future husband. Since I am sure he forgot his manners while escorting you to your room. My *other* son, Direk. Who will be like a brother to you I am sure."

I nod at them and acknowledge them for who they are and who they are to me. I try and look lovingly at Preston, but it's hard to do when he snakes his hand over my thigh and squeezes at just the right spot. Direk on the other hand winks at me and smiles like the sun.

"We are ready now Ms. Silver," Duke Laird announces. Striking up a conversation with Preston as soon as he is finished. I try to grab the attention of anyone to talk or to help with the serving, but no one seems to pay me any attention. Not even Direk. He has joined his father and brother in conversation.

The food being brought out looks delicious and smells even better. There is roast, potatoes, corn, a pastry I am unfamiliar with and some beans. Before I can even take my first bite, Duke Laird starts coughing. I look at him puzzled. Maybe he took to big of a bite and its stuck. Then as I go to help, Preston starts coughing as well. I start patting him on the back since he is closer. Nothing seems to help.

Soon we are over run with servants running to help Duke Laird and Preston. I call for one of them to run and grab a doctor, but they respond that he wont be near for another six months. I am at a loss of what to do.

Eventually the coughing dies down as the Duke and Preston start changing colors. First their normal pale skin, then blue, then purple then nothing. They fall out of their chairs and onto the floor. I gasp. Now what will I do? I can't marry Preston if he is dead.

The next thing I hear is laughter. Direk is laughing, like fully belly laughing. He turns to me and says, "Well that took less time than I thought. Now you are a Bastard Duke's Wife."

ABOUT THE AUTHOR

S.C. Winters has always been passionate about writing and storytelling. She describes herself as a curious author who loves exploring different themes and motifs. As part of their writing process, she loves immersing herself in their projects—diving headfirst into the research, production, and fine-tuning of the stories they feel are the most worthy of telling. From a young age she was always told that her flare for the fantasy and the dramatic would make for some amazing stories. With the encouragement of her family and friends she started writing. They rest as they say is history! She currently is living in Texas, with her husband and two dogs, Leia and Daisey. She also enjoys her time reading, writing and being outdoors.

FOLLOW S.C. WINTERS

Newsletter sign up:
https://wixsite.us2.list-manage.com/subscribe?u=b07abd8dc7127dce54c502aa9&id=5f67d21ba1

Amazon page link:
https://www.amazon.com/-/e/B089FPKWXS

Amazon author link:
https://www.amazon.com/author/scwinters

Instagram:
@s.c.winters

Facebook Page:
https://www.facebook.com/scwinters89/

Facebook Group:
https://www.facebook.com/groups/winterstorms/?ref=share

Facebook Profile:
https://www.facebook.com/scwinters4

Bookbub:
@authorscwinters

Website:
https://authorscwinters.wixsite.com/astormofbooks

SHE HAS A
DARK SECRET
SO DOES HE

Countessa Ksenia's
DARK SECRET

SCERINA ELIZABETH

COUNTESS KSENIA'S DARK SECRET
By Scerina Elizabeth

COPYRIGHT PAGE

Copyright © 2022 by Scerina Elizabeth
All rights reserved. This book or any portion thereof may not be reproduced or used in any manner whatsoever without the express written permission of the publisher except for the use of brief quotations in a book review.

Printed in the United States of America

First Printing, 2022

ASIN: B09GX8KYPH

Angelic Whispers Romance Anthologies

A MYSTERIOUS STRANGER

Staring out my cabin's tiny circular window, I started at the beautiful full moon. My thoughts drifting a million miles away to a place where I was unknown, and I was safe from those who wished to do me harm. The ship gently rocked as it sailed towards the new world that they called America, *"Land of the Free,"* they call it. It was where my new life awaited me, where not a soul knew who *or what* I was. I licked the warm blood of my latest victim off my lips, staring down at the lifeless body of the young man who tried to take advantage of me by force. A man who could not handle rejection met my deadly wraith. I was not like all the other creatures of my kind; I did not get pleasure out of killing. If anything, I felt for my victims, including those who were evildoers. My maker had taught me to always value human life because we all started out as humans at one point or another. We were in no shape or form superior to humanity, although there were those of my kind who felt as if we should be. These were the ones who lost their true humanity over time and became something else completely. The local villagers in my small village discovered what I was and were out for my blood. Had I not escaped when I did, I would be dead now. I was the last of my bloodline, a bloodline that held a very bloody history, especially within the village.

I was from the old country where they were very superstitious, and anyone who was different from them would be looked at under a microscope. I had just come home to settle my family estate after the passing of my father, The Count. The villagers believed my father and my entire family to be cursed and fed on human blood. They viewed us as vampires, and I can understand how we would look like vampires to an outsider. But we were not vampires; we were something else completely. Something much older and much wiser. True, we did feed on human blood for sustenance. We were also creatures of the night, but unlike vampires, we could walk in sunlight. If they really knew the truth about my kind, none of them would dare to cross paths with me or anyone from my family. We are more dangerous and deadlier than vampires. If the humans only knew the real truth about my kind, they would wish we were vampires as they are easier to kill.

I slowly licked the blood off of my tiny kitten-like fangs as I smiled at my reflection in the window. Thank God for an unknown deadly virus that was spreading all over the ship. No one would notice the missing passengers in which I fed off of. Naturally, they would assume it was the deadly virus that killed them, which worked out perfectly for me in the end. Keeping to myself and minding my own business, no one took notice of me…*or so I thought*. Unbeknownst to me, someone was closely watching me. I would soon find out I had a distant admirer who knew all about my dark secret. Someone who was not like me but another fellow creature of the night with a dark secret of their own. A dark secret that could get me killed in the very end if I did not play my cards right. Grabbing my tiny purse, I opened the cabin door and quietly slipped out, making my escape into the dark of the night. Walking quietly down the dark hallway, I sensed another presence nearby; they were not human. I felt my fangs grow as my vision darkened, and it transitioned to night vision. Picking up his scent, I turned slowly to face him.

"Who are you?" I demanded in a hiss.

"You need not worry about who I am. Just know I am a kindred spirit who is very much like you." He said.

"What do you mean?" I asked.

"Someone who has been watching and following you for a very long time." He replied.

I suddenly felt uneasy and vulnerable, "Are you stalking me?" I asked.

"No, if anything, I am an admirer who wishes only to get to know you better and be close to you." He said.

"Who are you?!" I asked, growing impatient and even more uneasy with each second that passed by.

"As I mentioned, you need not worry about me. Your secret is safe with me. My name is Peter Vladislav, and I been sent to watch over you," he said.

"Who sent you?" I asked.

"Your grandfather, Nikolai Petrovia," he replied, smiling at me warmly.

"Grandfather?" I asked confused, last I heard of the old man, he was dead. "How can this be? He is dead."

"He is not dead. He is waiting for you in the new world," Peter said.

Waving my hand as tears ran down my face and shaking my head, "Stop! Stop! Stop! What are you talking about? My grandfather is dead! I should know. I was the one who identified his body!" I cried out as tears flowed from my eyes.

"That was not your grandfather in the morgue that night. It was his twin brother who was my father, Antonio Petrovia," Peter replied.

"You mean to tell me all this time grandfather has been in America? Alive and well as the rest of us mourned his death, believing him to be dead?!" I asked incredulously.

"Yes," Peter replied.

"Why has no one reached out to any of us to tell us this?!" I asked.

"It was not safe; it still isn't safe. You are in grave danger. The man who killed my father is still at large. He is out to wipe out the entire Petrovia bloodline. He has no idea of me, only of you and that you are the last of the Petrovia," Peter said.

I looked at him. It was true. My family has been wiped out one by one by a mysterious assassin who we believed is a bounty hunter. He moved closer to me to wrap his arm around me. I suddenly felt as if someone had just walked over my grave. Looking up at him, I asked, "Why is it just now you come to me with news of my grandfather? Why did you not come sooner?"

"It was not safe. I had to wait till the time was right," he replied.

Looking deep into his eyes, I saw warmth and sincerity deep in them. He was telling the truth. I began to relax in his arms as we walked back to his cabin.

SANTUARY IN A STRANGER'S BED

The feel of his warm lips on my own lips stirred something deep inside of me. A kiss that started out so innocently soon became a kiss filled with such heat, passion, and desire that awakened the demoness deep within me. I needed more. I wanted more. I craved more than just his kiss alone. Growling deeply in my ears while he tore my blouse off, he whispered, "You awaken the beast deep inside of me." I felt my clit twitch with need and desire while he took my large breast into his hand and squeezed it firmly, making me cry out his name softly. Picking me up, he carries me over to the enormous bed in his cabin. Throwing me on his bed, he pulled me closer to the edge of the bed so that my ass was on the very edge, spreading my legs so that he could position himself in such a way that he was only mere inches away from my dripping wet throbbing pussy. Showing no mercy, he thrusted his tongue deep into my tight throbbing pussy, devouring me alive. Holding onto me tightly as I dug my long manicured nails deep into his scalp while he ate me out deeply, making me squirt over and over again. Whimpering softly, begging for more and more of his hot passion. My demoness was taking over as he made hot passionate love to me with just his tongue alone. Trying my best to keep that side of me hidden, but the urge was so strong and so powerful. I felt her slowly taking over my body and soul, but as I watched him, I could tell he, too, was changing. We both were in transition into our inner creatures. I watched as hair began to grow from his muscular back while the muscles on his back begun to contort and change into something else. His growls started to sound more guttural, like some kind of dangerous animal who was about to devour his prey alive. Within moments his body was covered in dark fur while I was no longer my human self but my inner creature who fed off of him. We fed off of each other as we made passionate love. A bond that connected us as a mate's bond that connected them for life.

We were fierce but beautiful creatures of the night making love to one another on our way to a new world in which I had never been before. A place where my grandfather sought refuge where no one knew him or of our kind. Where no one could do any harm to me. This new world held so much promise for a new life for me and our kind. We were not vampires, nor were we shifters or werewolves/lycanthropes. No, we were something else, much older and wiser. We were here long before the vampires, shifters, werewolves/lycanthropes came into existence. Some might say such creatures came from us, but in truth, we are in no shape or form associated or affiliated with them. We were Gods and Goddesses of the Moon Tribe called Faenyxia. We were part Fae, but we were not your normal Fae who was so full of light and love. We were much darker, dangerous, fiercer, and deadlier, yet we were very alluring and mesmerizing.

Together we came as the sun rose above the horizon, pulling me back in his arms. He held me close to him. Slowly we transition back into our human selves. Looking out the tiny cabin window, he said, "We will soon reach land."

Looking up at him, I asked, "How do you know?"

"I sense it. Your grandfather will be waiting for us when we arrive." He said, looking down at me, lightly stroking my hair.

I laid there in his arms, watching the waves gently splash against the window. The ship gently rocked back and forth, slowly lulling me to sleep.

Vampire vs. Fae

As I drifted off to sleep, a memory came to me…

I was back home in a time where my family was alive and so happy. A time when humans were not even aware of our kind, a time when we were truly safe and didn't need to flee. A time when my family was once true royalty and humans had the utmost respect for us. We always protected and looked over the humans of the local village who held such reverence for my family. This was no ordinary dream. It was, in fact, a memory that has always haunted me. It was the winter of 1876 during our annual Christmas Ball. It was a group of rogue feral vampires who attacked the local village. The local villagers turned on us and blamed us for the ruthless slayings of their neighbors and families. Some villagers always suspected us to be monsters who fed on the blood of humans. They even called us demons of the night. In less than a year, they manage to wipe out my family. I was the last of my bloodline, and I was caught during a feeding. The villagers who once loved and adored my family, especially me, who held such high respect for us and even viewed us as their guardian angels, now turned on us and were now out for my blood. I had no choice but to flee, seek refuge in this new land of America.

Looking back on that tragic night, we were all unaware of these rogue vampires who preyed on the local village. These rogue vampires were the start of vampirism and the world as I knew it was about to change and not for the better. These vampires were looking to run us out of our ancestral home, which was our true birthright. Although it was villagers that wiped out my family, I received word that vampirism was spreading across Europe like a deadly virus, wiping out my kind one by one. The vampires wanted to take our ancestral homes and place in history. They wanted to replace us. Some even turned some of us into their kind, creating a new breed. A hybrid of Fae and vampire called Faempyr. Some vampires even bred with our kind to create pure-blooded Faempyrs to strengthen their bloodlines and breed.

Dark Secrets Revealed

But I had a dark secret unknown to anyone else. There was another reason for me fleeing my country. I was pregnant with the King of Vampire's child. It was a boy. If he found out, he would keep me trapped within the walls of his dark Vampire Kingdom as his Fae Bride & Fae Queen. It was forbidden for my kind to intermingle with the vampires or any other species for that matter. The Vampire King had seduced me one night, even leading me to believe he was one of my kind. Falling prey to his seduction, he took me and impregnated me with his evil seed. I had to keep the father of my unborn son a secret; if my kind were to find out his father was, in fact, the Vampire King, it would mean certain death for both my unborn son and me.

Looking up at Peter, he was watching me with those dark, mysterious eyes of his. Sitting up, he said, "There is something I need to tell you."

Something flickered in his eyes, "What is it?" I asked. I sensed something was deeply troubling him.

"Truth is, I am not one of your kind," he said, raking his hand through his hair.

"What do you mean?" I asked, confused.

"You may not have heard of my kind, but we have always been around since the beginning of time. We are children of the wolf. Some call us lycanthropes which is our true name, but we are best known as werewolves." He said, looking at me with dark stormy eyes.

I looked at him, looking deep into his eyes, "You're serious, aren't you?" I asked. It was the first time I had ever heard of such a creature. I was only familiar with my kind and vampires, never werewolves or lycanthropes.

"Yes, I am very serious. Our kind have been trying to eradicate the vampires for millennia now, but with each millennium comes a new breed of vampire. Stronger than the previous generation. They are evolving into something else completely, something much stronger and untouchable. I was told that they were enemies of your kind. I came to your grandfather seeking assistance from him since he is King of your kind. He told me of a way to truly rid the world of vampires," he said, watching me before continuing, "In order for my kind to truly wipe out the vampire race, we would need to breed with your kind."

I looked at him, "It is forbidden for our kind to breed with another species. I find that hard to believe that my grandfather would allow such a thing!" I said, outraged. It almost looked and felt like an attempt of another species to take over our kind.

"Listen, I cannot fully explain it. Your grandfather can best explain it; I just know that our species must work together to wipe out the vampires, even if it means intermingling with each other and breeding purebloods to create an even stronger breed that is much stronger than the Faempyr breed. Our breed as one, a hybrid of both Werewolf and Fae, is much more powerful and stronger of the Faempyr breed. They wouldn't stand a chance against a purebred of our offspring. Werewolves have always been stronger than vampires, just imagine how much more stronger a hybrid of our kind would be?" He asked.

I listened to him, processing it all, unable to accept any of it. It was all so new to me. "I need to talk to my grandfather. None of this makes any sense," I said.

"He will explain it all when we arrive in America. He has a plan. He wants to return to Europe and reclaim your ancestral land and home. He wants your kind to reclaim Europe and restore it back to how it once was before vampires took over," Peter said.

I sense something else was deeply troubling him. He kept shifting uncomfortably. "What is it? What troubles you so? I sense there is something else going on," I said.

He looked at me, than turned away as if he was ashamed, reaching out. I turned his chin slowly towards me and said, 'It's okay, you can tell me."

Tears in his eyes, he begun to speak, "It is my family's fault why the vampires are out to rid the world of your kind. My family is out to rid the world of your kind and summoned the Vampire King to eradicate your kind. Before I was born, your kind wiped out the first of our kind and ever since than our kind have been seeking ways to eradicate your kind. But I am not like them, I have always loved your kind, my first bride was in fact a Fae. When my family found out her origins, they had her and my unborn child killed." He look down as tears flowed down his cheek.

I could not help but feel for him, although his family was at fault, he was an innocent bystander caught in the crossfire of this war between his kind and my kind. "Does my grandfather know of this?" I asked softly.

"No, I could not bring myself to tell him. I feared he would have me killed. So, please do not say a word of this to him. I am innocent in all of this." He pleaded.

"I won't say a word but my grandfather does need to know of this. You need to tell him." I said.

"I will, when the time is right." He promised.

As the words left his lips, we heard a loud crash and blood-curdling screams in the distance. The door flung open and a young man stood shouted "The ship has crashed. We need to abandon ship immediately!" he said with urgency in his voice.

TO BE CONTINUED…

A SPECIAL MESSAGE FROM SCERINA ELIZABETH

Dear Reader:

Stay tuned for the extended version of "Countessa Ksenia's Dark Secret" that is due to be release on the 11th of May 2022. This short story is only a sneak peek at what is to come in the extended version of this story. For more news and updates regarding the extended version of this story, subscribe to my newsletter on my official site at ScerinaElizabeth.NET.

Love Always,
Authoress Scerina Elizabeth.

ABOUT THE AUTHOR

SCERINA ELIZABETH
PARANORMAL ROMANCE EROTICA AUTHORESS

A Beautiful Disaster Just Waiting To Happen...

I have always had a creative imagination for as long as I could remember. Writing is a form of therapy for me for it is my escape from reality into my own little world where I can be creative. Writing has allowed me to be very expressive in my creativity.

A little bit about me. I love to read anything paranormal especially when romance is involved. I have always been a sucker for anything fantasy related. I suffer from severe depression and anxiety. Which can often effect my writing but I find ways to get around it. I have a wonderful support system within my group of author friends who experience the same thing as me. Such wonderful beautiful souls they truly are.

I love to hear from my readers and I love to interact with not just my readers but other authors as well. I look forward to hearing from anyone who enjoys my writing. It is true genuine fans who truly believe in my writing that make me the kind of writer that I am today. If it wasn't for them, I don't know where I would be today. So, I am truly thankful and grateful to all my true genuine fans.

FOLLOW SCERINA ELIZABETH

Official Author Site
http://www.scerinaelizabeth.net

Facebook
https://www.facebook.com/AuthoressScerinaElizabeth

Amazon
https://www.amazon.com/Scerina-Elizabeth/e/B071HXM584/

Goodreads
https://www.goodreads.com/author/show/16805176.Scerina_Elizabeth

Bookbub
https://www.bookbub.com/profile/scerina-elizabeth

Twitter
https://twitter.com/ScerinaElizaNET